Mathias Franey,
Powder Monkey

By Ellen W. Leroe

Illustrated by Sarah S. Brannen

Text copyright © 2011 by Ellen W. Leroe
Illustrations copyright © 2011 by Sarah S. Brannen

All rights reserved. No part of this book may be reproduced in any form without permission in writing from the publisher, except by a reviewer who may quote brief passages in a review.

First published in the United States of America by:

Twin Lights Publishers, Inc.
8 Hale Street
Rockport, Massachusetts 01966
Telephone: (978) 546-7398
http://www.twinlightspub.com

ISBN: 1-934907-04-9
ISBN: 978-1-934907-04-7

10 9 8 7 6 5 4 3 2 1

Acknowledgment
Many thanks to Matthew Brenckle and Rebecca Parmer at the USS Constitution Museum for their invaluable help and advice on sailors' clothing, ship's rigging, and life aboard the *Constitution* in 1812.

Book design by
SYP Design & Production, Inc.
http://www.sypdesign.com

Printed in China

— DEDICATIONS —

To the courageous powder monkeys who
served on the USS *Constitution*

Ellen W. Leroe

To Katherine

Sarah S. Brannen

Mathias scrambled up the rigging of the USS *Constitution*. Be careful, he warned himself. One slip and he'd tumble off the ship into the deep water below.

His good friend, James, gripped the ropes next to him.

"Think we'll be spotting a British man-of-war today, Minnow?" James asked with a grin.

Mathias swallowed. He didn't like to think of that. He also didn't like being called Minnow, just because he was the smallest boy on board. But once another boy, Crocker, started teasing him, the name stuck.

"Jack Mitchell says that there's been talk of war," Mathias said. "He's angry over the English boarding American ships and capturing our men."

James let out a whoop. "I say we fight!"

But Mathias didn't answer. He and the other powder monkeys, boys who brought ammunition to the gunners, had only drilled in combat situations. It was scary to think of the *Constitution* facing enemy ships.

A bos'n's pipe sounded.

"All hands on deck," James cried. "I wonder what's happening."

The boys scrambled down the rigging. There were tense expressions on some of the officers' faces, and Mathias knew they were about to hear something important.

The four hundred and fifty members of the crew assembled quickly on deck. Mathias and James joined the other powder monkeys, shoving and joking.

"Here, now, none of this larking about," Master-at-Arms Henry Owens ordered.

Everyone settled down.

Mathias caught the eye of his friend, Jack Mitchell, the second captain of the foretop. Jack nodded at him, and smiled. Someday I'd like to join Jack at the very top of the ship, Mathias thought. But that took courage, maybe more than he had.

Third Lieutenant George Read stepped forward. "Men, I have a declaration for you to hear."

The entire crew immediately straightened. As he began reading, Mathias and James exchanged startled glances.

The United States was now officially at war with Great Britain as of June 18, 1812. At *war*, Mathias whispered under his breath.

"England's been bullying America long enough," Lieutenant Read said.

"Aye, ten years," Jack shouted.

Mr. German, a midshipman, stepped forward. "Sir, will you give us permission to cheer?"

Lieutenant Read nodded his head.

"Nine cheers, men!" Mr. German cried.

A minnow can be small, but mighty, Mathias vowed. He raised his voice along with the others.

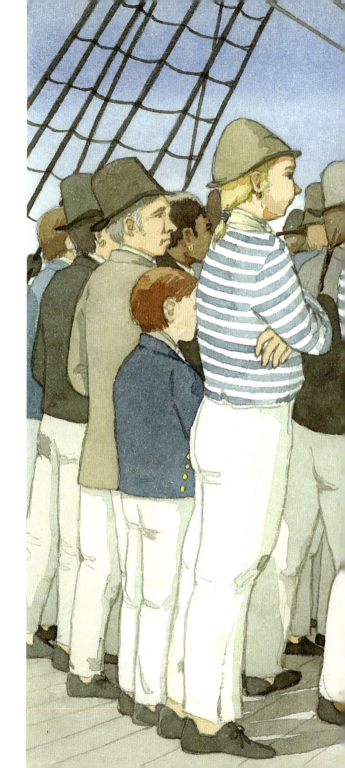

In the following days Mathias drilled with the great guns. He knew what he had to do, and tried to keep up with the other powder monkeys.

First, he reported to his station, Long Gun, No. 11. The long gun was a nine-foot-long cannon. It was so heavy it took nine to fourteen men to work a system of ropes and pulleys to roll it in and out of the gun port.

"Get here quicker," one of the gun crew sharply said.

"Minnow's not as fast as me," Crocker boasted, running past Mathias.

Mathias frowned and picked up the leather bucket called a pass box. He hurried across the crowded gun deck to reach the main hatch.

When he reached the main hatch, he handed the empty pass box to a waiting crew member and received a full one in return. Inside were bags of powder called cartridges. Men formed a human chain throughout the ship to pass the ammunition.

Mathias delivered the cartridge to the man who loaded the cannon.

Then Mathias grabbed the empty box and dashed to the main hatch. Once he exchanged it for another full box, he hurried back to his station—and did it all over again.

He knew the drill. But could he perform under fire?

It was a mild, cloudy afternoon, August 19.

Mathias scrubbed the sand-covered area around the cannon, while Crocker and David worked nearby.

"Put some muscle into that, monkey!" Mr. Owens squinted down at Mathias.

As Mathias used more force, Crocker glanced over and snickered.

"Sail ho!" a lookout from the tops shouted.

The men on deck ran to the rails. Excitement rippled through Mathias as he kept scrubbing. For weeks they had been hoping to find British warships. Had they finally found one?

Captain Hull, First Lieutenant Charles Morris, and Sailing Master John Aylwin came topside. Captain Hull sent Mr. German aloft with the spyglass.

"She's a great vessel, sir," Mr. German reported. "Tremendous sails."

"Call all hands," commanded Captain Hull.

Mathias and James raced over to the rail. They squeezed in between Mr. Adams, the boatswain, and Moses Smith, a friendly sailor.

"We're in for it now," Mr. Adams stated.

"Aye," Moses agreed. "This is a fight that'll prove our honor."

"But we've never been in battle," Mathias said.

Mr. Adams thumped the rail. "The *Constitution* is the largest, fastest fighting ship of her class. Her guns will do the talking, never fear."

Mathias hoped he was right.

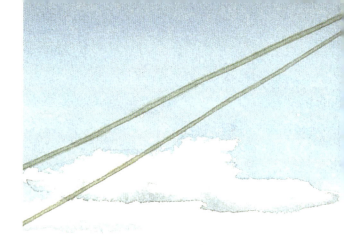

The *Constitution* chased the unknown ship for an hour and a half. Mathias finished cleaning the long gun, and two others, and then delivered messages to officers.

As the sun dropped in the hazy sky, Mathias found a brief moment to rest. He stopped by the stove on the gun deck. No one was there, and the galley fires had been put out. But Cook's pet, a tan-and-white-coated cat, padded over to Mathias.

"Hey there, Scamp," Mathias said. He bent down and scratched behind the cat's ears. "I wish you belonged to me."

Mathias remembered his own dog, Buster, and suddenly missed his family. When he spotted the notice to enlist on the *Constitution* in April of last year, his parents had been dead against it.

"You're too young," his mother had cried.

"I'm old enough," Mathias stubbornly said.

"A lad your size, do you know what you're getting into?" his father had demanded. "There's hard work ahead of you serving on a ship."

"I want to do it," Mathias insisted.

His father had finally given in. "Maybe you know best. If anything will make a man of you, it's facing action and danger onboard a frigate."

And now by nightfall, Mathias would find out.

"We're gaining on her!" James cried ten minutes later.

"Aye, and she's not running," Moses said, staring across the water. "She wants to fight."

Mathias hopped from foot to foot. "Is it the *Guerriere*?"

For weeks men had talked about meeting up with the 38-gun frigate.

Moses scratched his head. "She hasn't raised her ensigns yet. But I believe it could be a British warship."

Earlier, Captain Hull had ordered all his light sails in, and shouted: "Clear the decks for action!"

It was now time for battle.

"Are you ready, Minnow?" James asked.

Mathias nodded. In spite of his fears, he felt a rising excitement.

The drummers began a steady roll, the signal it was time to fight. The entire crew raced barefoot to their stations, ready to fire the guns in combat for their first battle. Everything was prepared. Mathias saw the tubs of water, needed for putting out fires, or helping the thirsty gunners. The decks had been wet and then sanded.

"It's to prevent you boys from slipping as you carry the gunpowder," Mr. Owens explained.

Crocker nudged Mathias. "It's to soak up all the blood, Minnow. Could be yours."

Mathias knew their work was dangerous, but they had to fight for America.

By 4:45 P.M. every crew member on the *Constitution* was in his place. Mathias was, too. He waited by Long Gun, Number 11. All thirteen men were shirtless in the heat. They wore handkerchiefs tied around their ears to block the cannon roar once they started firing.

The shutters of the gun ports opened, letting in shafts of hazy sun. About a half mile away, the enemy ship swung and turned. They're moving into firing range, Mathias thought. His stomach tightened.

"She's carrying big guns," Gun Captain Mahoney said. He patted the black cannon. "We'll soon give her a taste of ours."

A cry went up along the deck.

"She's hoisted her colors," someone shouted. "It's the *Guerriere*, right enough!"

Mathias closed his eyes. He wasn't much for praying, but he said a little prayer now.

Just for a moment, all was still. From across the water he could hear the drums of the *Guerriere*, and rattle of their muskets and swords.

Gun Captain Mahoney pointed at Mathias. "Bring us some powder, and don't you dawdle."

Mathias grabbed the two pass boxes and hurried away.

"Be fast," he whispered, "and remember the drill."

He dodged around other running boys as they all made for the main hatch. At one point he stumbled. One of the pass boxes dropped. Luckily, it was James coming behind him, and not Crocker or David. The two boys would have laughed and said a minnow was too tiny to be a powder monkey.

Mathias picked up the box, more determined than ever to do a good job. He avoided looking at the other fourteen gun crews that lined the side of the deck. He tried not to think about what would happen once the *Guerriere* fired on them. He had one job and one job only, bring empty pass boxes to the main hatch and receive full ones in return. Then race as quick as he could back to his gun crew who waited anxiously for the ammunition.

"Without powder the guns are useless," Mr. Owens had told Mathias and the boys.

The *Guerriere* could start firing at any moment. The *Constitution* had to be ready to fire back. Faster, Mathias kept saying. Faster.

His men were waiting.

Mathias delivered the cartridges to the gun crew.

Gun Captain Mahoney thumped the cannon. "This beast needs more fighting power, Mathias. Bring us some more, on the double."

Mathias didn't hesitate. He raced back and forth to the hatch many times, passing the other powder monkeys. No one talked. No one joked. They were too intent on their work. Mathias's heart was pounding with nervous excitement, but he never stopped.

When the cannons were all prepared, Mathias waited with the gun crew. A dead quiet dropped on the deck. The men were tense, eyes focused on the *Guerriere*. With a shocking roar, the British ship fired all its guns on the starboard side.

Mathias jumped when two cannon balls slammed into the hull. The *Constitution* shook.

Captain Hull ordered Lieutenant Charles Morris to raise their flags, an invitation to battle. The *Guerriere* continued to fire her cannons. Rounds hit the foremast, and pounded the hull.

"Why aren't we fighting back?" Mathias said.

"Soon," one of the gun crew said. "We need to get closer."

Less than ten minutes later, Captain Hull gave the command. In a carrying voice he shouted: "Now boys, hull her!"

The *Constitution*'s full battery of guns boomed.

The cannons on the gun deck roared. They jerked from the recoil, and the *Constitution* rolled hard. Mathias fell and let out a soft cry.

"*Guerriere*'s taken a direct hit!" a gunner yelled. "Her hull and rigging are cut!"

"More powder!" Gun Captain Mahoney ordered.

Mathias jumped to his feet and grabbed the boxes. He raced back and forth to the main hatch in a sea of noise, cannon blasts, and yelling. The guns went off non-stop. The *Constitution* shifted and rolled with each broadside. The men cheered, as *Guerriere*'s mizzenmast toppled. Mathias heard screams of pain, as well, from the dying and wounded on both ships.

There was a ferocious crash as *Guerriere*'s bowsprit tangled itself in *Constitution*'s mizzen rigging. Mathias felt the ship shudder and heard men shouting on the quarterdeck above. Through the openings of the gun port Mathias looked directly across at the *Guerriere*. The ships were so close he could stare directly into the faces of the gun crew on the British warship. The emotion and hatred in their eyes was like nothing he had ever seen before.

Mathias froze. He trembled so hard the boxes were shaking.

Mr. Owens stopped as he was hurrying past. He stared into Mathias's eyes.

"Don't be afraid, lad," he said. "Now do your ship proud."

Mathias nodded. He tightened his grip on the pass boxes and took off again.

The battle raged on. The faces and bodies of the gunners were blackened from gunpowder. Like a well-drilled team they obeyed Gun Captain Mahoney as he called the actions for firing: "Stop vent! Sponge! Load! Run out your guns!"

Mathias continued to bring cartridges to his station. "Do your ship proud," he whispered.

Mr. Owens ordered him to pass a message along to Lieutenant Morris.

Up on the quarterdeck he blinked from the fiery glare of *Guerriere*'s cannon bursts.

The *Constitution* shook as balls pounded her hull and then bounced off.

"Huzza!" someone cried in the smoke-filled air. "Her sides are made of iron!"

The *Constitution* fired broadside after broadside, and the *Guerriere* was damaged. But the British warship continued to fight. Mathias found Lieutenant Morris and delivered his message. Before he ran below to the gun deck, he heard men shouting.

"Our flag's been shot!" An alarmed officer pointed to the mast.

Mathias stopped along with the other men to look up. The *Constitution*'s jack, a blue flag with a circle of white stars, was no longer aloft in the wind. It had gotten tangled with the rigging.

"They'll think we've struck our colors and surrendered," someone cried.

Without hesitating, Mathias jumped onto the rigging and began climbing. He had to reach the flag.

A man tugged at his leg. "No, boy."

But others encouraged him.

Mathias blocked it all out as he jumped onto the topgallant mast. It was easy for him to wrap his legs around the wood and move quickly.

A minnow can climb a mast, he told himself. Keep going.

Now he could hear men on the *Guerriere* shout that they could see him. Mathias knew they'd do anything in their power to prevent him from reaching the *Constitution*'s flag.

In the cloudy darkness of battle smoke, cannons exploded on both ships. The mast shuddered and jerked. Mathias swayed and held on tightly. When the smoke cleared from the blasts, Mathias glanced over at the *Guerriere*. Sharpshooters standing on a platform on a mast raised muskets and took aim.

Zing! Zing! Bullets whizzed by, just missing him. Mathias shook off his fears and reached the top. He plucked the fallen flag from the rigging and tied it securely around the mast. He made sure it was attached tightly so it couldn't drop again. The jack fluttered, then lifted proudly in the wind.

As men below cheered, Mathias began to work his way down.

"Well done, lad," an officer said, when Mathias hit the deck. He clapped him on the back. "Now return to your duties."

There was no time to stand idle. The battle between the two ships continued. Mathias hurried to his station.

Gun Captain Mahoney pointed to the empty boxes. "Fill those up, and be quick!"

Mathias raced to obey. When he returned with the gunpowder, he learned that Lieutenant Bush had been killed and Lieutenant Morris badly wounded. And then the horrifying shouts of "Fire! Fire!" rang through the ship.

"No man leaves his station," Gun Captain Mahoney ordered. "It'll soon be doused."

Mathias raced to the main hatch to pick up a full pass box. When he ran back to his station, the men wore triumphant grins.

"*Guerriere*'s foremast and mainmast are destroyed," one cried. "She's taking on water, fast."

Cannon blasts grew less frequent. Through the open gun ports, Mathias could hear the sounds of wounded and dying men in pain. He hoped it would be over soon. Finally, just twenty-five minutes after *Constitution* fired its first broadside, the British man-of-war surrendered.

"We've beaten England's finest," Gun Captain Mahoney announced to his men.

Mathias joined in the cheers.

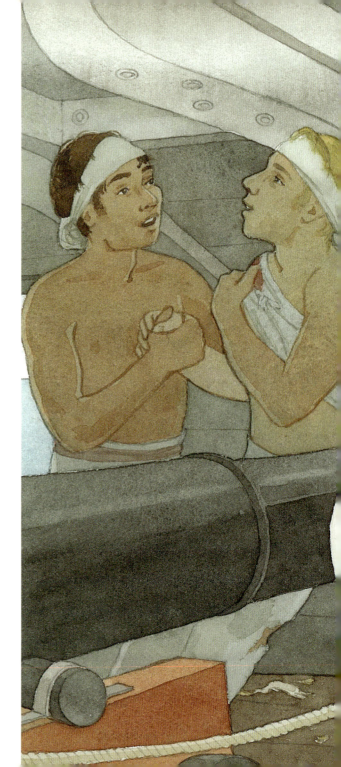

"Here, you two powder monkeys, straighten the deck," Mr. Owens ordered.

The battle was over, but general clean-up and repairs had just begun.

Mathias and James set to work, picking up big splinters and bits of rigging blasted by *Guerriere*'s cannon balls. After that was done, they got on their knees to wash the mixture of sand and blood off the deck.

"I heard Mr. Morris is badly wounded," Mathias said softly.

Moses Smith walked by. "Don't you worry, lads, he'll be right as rain."

"What about the rest of our crew?" James asked.

Moses looked out over the water. "There are seven dead and seven wounded. But lots more killed on *Guerriere*. We'll be sending boats later to pick up their men."

Crocker, David and two other boys joined to help with the clean-up. Jack Mitchell came up to Mathias. He laid a hand on his shoulder.

"You finally climbed to the top of the masts, lad," he said. "That was brave work raising our flag."

Crocker stared at Mathias in shock. "Minnow did that?"

"No more Minnow," Jack corrected. "He was more like a Man-of-War by that deed."

Mathias flushed with pride when Jack turned and walked away.

Mathias thought about Jack's comment for the rest of the evening. He may have been the smallest boy in the entire crew, but he had shown a Man-of-War fighting spirit. And that was something to be proud of.

Up top, he and James watched the boats return with British prisoners.

"You missed *Guerriere*'s captain coming aboard earlier," Moses said, joining them.

"And none too pleased was Captain Dacres, I wager, to be visiting Old Ironsides as the losing officer."

"Old Ironsides?" Mathias said. "What's that?"

Moses threw back his head and laughed. "Didn't their cannon balls harmlessly bounce off *Constitution*'s thick wooden sides as if they were iron? She was christened proper-like today!"

That evening as he settled in his hammock, Mathias thought about how an untested American ship had gone head-to-head with the mighty British navy, and proved to be a first-class power. And he and the rest of the powder monkeys had helped in that victory.

All in all, he reflected sleepily, it had been a good day—

"G'night, James," he called softly to his friend in the hammock beside him.

"G'night, Mathias," James replied.

"G'night, Mathias," the other boys said.

(No more Minnow!, Mathias rejoiced!)

—a very good day.

A Note to The Reader

The USS *Constitution* won a major naval victory when she defeated the British warship HMS *Guerriere* on August 19, 1812. The incidents that happened during the historic battle are recorded fact, and about 20 boys of different ages served as powder monkeys during this encounter.

Mathias Franey, James Howe, David Blanchard, and Crocker Hardin were the names of real boys who ran powder cartridges to the men working the gun stations. There is nothing known about the individual actions of the boys, so I used my imagination in creating what I thought they might have said, done, and felt during their first exciting battle. A young man really did climb to the foremast of the *Constitution* to attach the flag more securely, but his name was Daniel Hogan.

After the victory, Captain Isaac Hull wrote to the Secretary of the Navy, Paul Hamilton, on August 28, 1812. In his letter describing the battle, Captain Hill reports how proud he was of his men: "…they all fought with great bravery; and it gives me great pleasure to say that from the smallest boy in the ship to the oldest seaman not a look of fear was seen." Mathias "minnow" Franey proved his courage during this historic fight, as did the rest of the powder monkeys.

More about Powder Monkeys

Being a powder monkey aboard a warship like the USS *Constitution* was dangerous, exciting, and serious work. Firing the heavy long guns and shorter 4-foot "smashers," or carronades, required crews of seven to fourteen men ---and at least one powder monkey. Powder monkeys didn't have the strength to load, aim, and fire the heavy cannons. But they were fast. They went barefoot so they could easily run back and forth from the hatches with the bags of powder (or cartridges) contained in a leather tube slung over their shoulders. A powder monkey not only had to be quick-footed, but careful. During a battle, the crew fired pistols and muskets. One flying spark could strike the leather tube, igniting the gunpowder, and injuring or killing the boy. A powder monkey's work was dangerous!

Many other crew members worked together to help the powder monkeys in supplying the cannons with ammunition. The ammunition on the *Constitution* was stored in the powder room, or magazine, situated deep in the hold of the ship. To get the gunpowder from the powder room to the gun deck, teams of men lined up on each deck to pass the cartridges from hand to hand in one continuous chain. Some crew members were stationed at hatchways to pass the gunpowder up to the next deck. Powder monkeys would race to the main hatch on the gun deck to receive the cartridges from these men.

Powder monkeys had other duties besides running the gunpowder to the men firing the cannons. They were rated Boy, the lowest level on board a ship, and paid $6 a month. Because of this, they had many unpleasant tasks to perform. When the *Constitution* wasn't fighting a British Man-of-War, powder monkeys washed clothes and scrubbed the decks, cleaned the pens where livestock was kept, or helped the cook in the galley. They passed messages to officers or other crew members. They climbed the rigging to adjust the sails. When their work was done, they could relax with the other boys, sing sea chanteys with the crew, or play with the few pets on board. At night, they slept in hammocks in a separate part of the ship, away from the rest of the crew. They used their rolled-up clothes as pillows.

No one is certain when British ships first began using powder monkeys, but some experts believe it was as early as the fifteenth century. If there were heavy cannons to be fired, then small boys would be needed to bring gunpowder to the men. But not all powder monkeys were boys. Sometimes women or older men helped with these duties if they were on board during a naval battle. In contrast, women were not allowed on American warships, and in 1812 most of the monkeys on the *Constitution* were older men.

Powder monkeys are often overlooked for their role in assisting the crew of a U.S. Navy ship, but several were wounded and even killed in combat. And some proved so brave and courageous doing their duty during the Civil War that they were awarded the Medal of Honor. The boys who served as powder monkeys may have been young, but their actions during battle proved they were heroes in their own small, but important way.

Glossary of Ship Terms

"All hands on deck"
Every person onboard must report to the ship's main deck.

Battery
All the guns on one deck.

Boatswain (bos'n)
A skilled seaman in charge of the ship's anchors, rigging, sails, and hull.

Broadside
A firing of all the ship's guns on one side.

Colors
See "Jack"

"Drums beat the men to quarters"
Send men to their posts at the roll of a drum in readiness for a battle.

Ensign
A flag flown by a ship that displays their nationality.

Flying jib
A small triangular sail in front of the ship.

Foremast
The mast at the front of the ship.

Foretop
The platform at the head of a ship's foremast.

Frigate
A square-rigged vessel of war, carrying guns on one covered deck.

Gun port
An opening in a ship for the front of a cannon.

Hatchway
A passageway with stairs or ladders leading to an enclosed space on a ship.

Hull
The frame or body of a ship.

"Hull her!"
Command to fire cannon balls into the hull of a ship to cause damage.

"Huzza!"
A cheer, like "Hooray!"

Jack
American Jack, a small blue flag with a star for each state, flown on a ship.

Long gun
A muzzle-loading, long-barreled cannon capable of firing a solid shot weighing 24 pounds, with a range of about 1200 yards.

Magazine
A room with stored cartridges and gunpowder located below the waterline of a ship.

Mainmast
A mast in the middle of a ship.

Man-of-War
A warship.

Midshipman
A young officer-in-training.

Minnow
A small fish.

Musket
A heavy, large-caliber shoulder firearm.

Powder room
See "Magazine."

Rigging
All the lines on a ship that support the masts, and also work in setting and taking in sails.

Sniper
Expert shooter who fires on exposed people from a hidden location.

Starboard
The right side of a ship when facing forward.

Staysails
A triangular sail set between two masts.

"Stop vent, sponge, load, run out your guns"
The actions that different men performed in order to fire the cannon: 1) stop (or cover) the vent, a hole in the back of the cannon; 2) push gunpowder inside the barrel, then the round shot or cannon ball; 3) poke a stiff wire through the vent to pierce the sack of gunpowder; 4) add more powder and light the powder with a slow match, and...BOOM!

"Strike the colors"
To lower the flag on a ship, as a show of surrender.

Top gallant
The mast or sail on a ship above the topmast.

Ellen W. Leroe

Ellen W. Leroe created her first picture book at the age of seven, and has been writing ever since. Growing up in New Jersey, she now lives in San Francisco with fantastic views of the water and the Bay Bridge from her office. She's written over thirty books for children of all ages, and considers that play, and not work. Other loves include reading for hours, collecting tiny typewriters, exercising faithfully, and taking long walks around the city. There's more information about Ellen at www.ellenleroe.com.

Sarah S. Brannen

Sarah S. Brannen is the author and illustrator of *Uncle Bobby's Wedding* (G.P. Putnam's Sons, 2008). Sarah also illustrated *The ABC Book of American Homes* (Charlesbridge Publishing, 2008) and *Digging for Troy* (Charlesbridge, 2011). Her illustrations also appear in several children's magazines. Sarah lives in Massachusetts. To learn more about her books, visit www.sarahbrannen.com.

	DATE DUE		

E
LER

327E3000309064
Leroe, Ellen.

Mathias Franey,
powder monkey

JAMES HENNIGAN ELEM SCHOOL
BOSTON PUBLIC SCHOOLS

411151 01695 22043A 22085E   0002